The Hungry Anteater

Copyright ©1991 by Paul Dowling.
This paperback edition first published in 2001 by Andersen Press Ltd. The rights of Paul Dowling to be identified as the author and illustrator of this work have been asserted by him in accordance with the Copyright, Designs and Patents Act, 1988.
First published in Great Britain in 1991 by Andersen Press Ltd., 20 Vauxhall Bridge Road, London SW1V 2SA.
Published in Australia by Random House Australia Pty., 20 Alfred Street, Milsons Point, Sydney, NSW 2061.
All rights reserved. Colour separated in Switzerland by Photolitho AG, Zurich.
Printed and bound in China.

10 9 8 7 6 5 4 3 2 1

British Library Cataloguing in Publication Data available.

ISBN 0 86264 345 7

This book has been printed on acid-free paper

The Hungry Anteater

by Paul Dowling

Andersen Press · London

"Have you got any ants?"
said the hungry anteater.
"I'm starving."
   "Not me," said the creature.
"I'm an encyclopaedia eater. I
only eat encyclopaedias.
Here have a page."

The anteater looked down the page.

Antelope
A fabulous horned beast.

Antique
A very old object like this silver candelabrum.

Antler
A hat worn by a deer

He scratched his head
and turned the page over.

It looked like an ant.

He sniffed it.

He poked his
tongue out at it.

Ant
Hymenopterous formicadae

A small insect, delicious
with potatoes and gravy
(often found in pants).

He licked it.
"Yurrk!" he said.

Round the corner he met a creature
sucking sticky tape.
"Have you got any ants?" he said.

"Not me pal," said the creature. "I'm a
sticky tape sucker. I sit on my sunlounger
with my shades on and suck sticky tape.
Go on, have a suck."

The anteater sucked some sticky tape,
but the sticky tape got stuck to his long
sticky tongue.

He got into a terrible tacky tangle.

"I think I'll stick to ants," he said.

Walking down the street was a creature gobbling umbrellas.

"Have you got any ants?" said the anteater. "I'm famished."

"Oh, no!" said the creature. "I'm an umbrella gobbler. I only gobble umbrellas. Here gobble one!"

The anteater gobbled an umbrella.

He gobbled it sideways,
but it was too wide.

He gobbled it frontways,

but the umbrella
suddenly opened,

and when he tried
to close it again,
the umbrella gobbled
him!
   "Oh lick, stick
and gobble!" cried
the anteater . . .

"HAS ANYONE GOT ANY ANTS?"

"Not me," said the nasturtium nibbler.
"I only nibble nasturtiums."

"Not me," said the personal computer
chewer. "I only chew personal computers."

"Not me," said the supermarket trolley swallower. "I only swallow supermarket trolleys."

"Not me," said the walking stick licker.
"I only lick walking sticks."

"But I have," said a creature not eating
anything at all. "I've got lots of ants. Follow me."

The anteater followed the creature
through a puddle, along a path, in and
out of trees, past a cheeseburger van,

across a river, up twenty-two steps to a door.
"Phew!" said the anteater.
The creature opened the door.

The anteater couldn't believe his eyes. There right in front of him was an enormous ant-hill, jam packed with fresh juicy ants.

"Tuck in," said the creature.

The anteater dived in

and stuffed himself with scrumptious ants.

"Slurp . . . gomf . . .
schlup . . . munch . . .
how come . . .
thlurp . . .
you've got a
super stock of
scrumpy . . .
shlump . . .
ants?" he said. "What do
you munch for your
meals? . . . burp"

"What me?" said
the creature.

"I don't eat a lot.

. . . I'm an anteater eater!"

...and I'm an
ANTEATER
EATER EATER!